MYRIAD BOOKS LIMITED
35 Bishopsthorpe Road, London SE26 4PA

First published in 2005 by
MIJADE PUBLICATIONS
16-18, rue de l'Ouvrage
5000 Namur-Belgium

© Emilie Vanvolsem, 2005

Translation: Lisa Pritchard

ISBN 1 84746 030 5

Printed in China

That's quite enough!

By Emilie Vanvolsem

MYRIAD BOOKS LIMITED

Hi! My name is Casper and…
aaaaaAAAchoo!
Oh no! I've got the sneezes again.
All that dust makes me itch and
sneeze…
Aaaachoooo!

Sniff... sniff
I live with the Smiths.
They are a really nice family
but they're very messy.
Aaaachoooo!

I look after the house when they go out.

Uh-oh! What's that noise?
Someone's at the door.
They're trying to get in!
Aaaachoooo!

Heeeeeeeeelp!
It's a scary monster!
Aaaachoooo!

What is it? A Martian? A spy? An ogre?
Maybe it's a witch who'll turn me into a mouse?
Oh no!

I'd better hide.

But the monster is coming to get me.

"Ohmylookatallthosepawprints!" it shrieks.

Even when I hide in the bathroom the monster finds me. And this time it's squirting something horrible. Do you think it's poison?

Phew! The monster won't find me here.
It's too busy pretending it's a ghost.

I'm very sleepy. Now I can see the monster,
and it doesn't look so scary. I think it's hunting spiders.

I don't think it's a monster or a witch.
Look, it's chasing flies. It's not got any
claws, just that special fluffy thing.

Oh wow! Am I dreaming?
Look what it's put in my bowl!
My favourite… **mmmmm.**

What a relief! It's not a monster after all –
and guess what? I've stopped sneezing. And
all because of our lovely house fairy.

Purr... purrr... purrrrr...